W9-AAH-624

Jack and Jill
went up the hill

Dickery, dickery, dare,
The Pig flew up in the air

I saw a ship a-sailing

Hush-a-bye, baby, on the tree-top

Baa, baa, black sheep

Rain, rain go away

Hark! hark! the dogs bark

Ding, dong, bell
The cat is in the well!

Ring a-round a
rosie,
a pocket full of
posie

Twinkle, twinkle, little star